BLOOD DIARIES

TALES OF A 6TH-GRADE VAMPIRE

BY EDGAR STOKER
(EXCEPT REALLY BY MARISSA MOSS)

LIBRARY OF CONGRESS CATALOG NUMBER 2013038641

TEXT AND ILLUSTRATIONS COPYRIGHT 2014 MARISSA MOSS
BOOK DESIGN BY SIMON STAHL
FONTS BY BRADLEY NELSON, RICH GAST, AND RAY LARABIE

PUBLISHED IN 2014 BY CRESTON BOOKS IN BERKELEY, CALIFORNIA
PRINTED IN THE USA ON SUSTAINABLY SOURCED PAPER

1 2 3 4 5 666 4 8 9 10

FSC
www.fsc.org
MIX
From responsible sources
FSC® C002589

To Kristen,
who knows what it's like to live in two different worlds,
welcome to the vampire clan!

January 1

My name is Edgar and I'm a vampire. Kidding! I just have very sharp teeth. No, that's not true. Well, it is true, I do have sharp teeth. But that's because I AM a vampire. Really. Only the thing is, it's a secret.

Obviously my family knows. They're all vampires, too - Mom, Dad, Grandmother, Grandfather, Granny, Gramps, great-grandparents, great-great-grandparents, great-great-great-grandparents (you get the idea), all my aunts and uncles and cousins. But the kids at school don't know. And according to my parents, they can't know, not ever.

I've heard this lecture for as long as I can remember.

Grandfather
↓

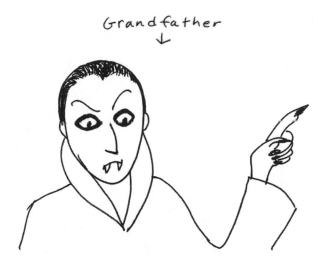

"If a mortal discovers our true nature, there will be a vicious mob at our doors, armed with stakes and torches. It's happened before and it can happen again. A couple of centuries ago, Cousin Julius bit a dog in the park - the stupid fool couldn't wait until dark. He was too hungry, and the dog smelled delicious, like the kind you would slurp up slathered with onions and relish.

"A man strolling by saw Julius with fangs bared and raised such a ruckus, you wouldn't believe! Julius flew home, but it was too late, word was out.

"When it was over, all that was left of Julius was a pile of garlic-covered ashes."

Grandfather always leans forward and stares at me with his glittering cold eyes whenever he comes to the end of the story.

"And that's why," he grills the moral into me, "that's why we may walk among mortals, but we can NEVER trust them. They're never our friends!"

The reason I'm writing this stuff down, the reason I'm keeping a diary, which is kind of a human thing to do, is because of my other grandfather, the one I call Gramps.

He's the one who gave me this book for Winter Solstice. Of course, we don't celebrate Christmas. Everyone knows what happens when vampires get near a crucifix.

And we don't care what anyone says, it's still a Christian holiday, no matter how commercial it's become. Take away the ribbons, wrapping paper, tree, lights, ornaments, and it's one big birthday party for Unmentionable. So naturally we avoid it as much as we can. Used to be that's when vampires would go on holiday, touring bat caves and taking long night hikes, but now that we're trying to blend in, to be more human-like, we have our own shadow holiday of Winter Solstice.

Plus a lot of vampire kids were feeling left out, like the whole world was having a party except us. Mom and dad vampires worried that their kids would start celebrating Christmas on the sly,

making friends with humans so they could help dec-
orate a tree. To lure kids back to the purity of
vampire ways, we came up with our own holiday, no
fancy lights or ornaments involved.

Instead we get together for a big blood
feast, our one time a year when we can drink fresh
blood. Not from humans, of course, that hasn't been
allowed since the Edict of 1922. Now we rely on
blood banks for human blood, which is still pretty
tasty even if it's been frozen or freeze-dried. I'm
not keen on canned blood (that icky metallic after-
taste), but the fresh-from-concentrate (meaning
not really fresh at all) is not bad.

For truly fresh blood, though, we can only
bite animals, and even that only on special holidays,
like Solstice. We gather a big herd of goats, sheep,

cows, pigs, maybe a turkey or two. Kind of like the festival of Eid al-Adha in Islam, where every household sacrifices a cow, camel, sheep, or goat in remembrance of Abraham being willing to sacrifice his son Isaac, but in the end killing a goat instead.

Me, I'm partial to pigs. I'll take a fat, juicy hog over a stringy, tough goat any day. And I'm not a big fan of camel meat, either. Too lumpy.

Lucky for me, this year was a really good year for pigs. There were plenty of them, so I didn't have to fight off any of my cousins to get one. I got a nice pink piglet all to myself!

And this diary. Giving presents is another

human thing, something vampires don't usually do. But like Gramps says, we want to fit in better with humans, camouflaged in a way, so acting a little human is a good idea. Besides this isn't really a present - it's a job, a kind of assignment.

This is what Gramps said:

"Edgar, this is a serious task I ask of you! Vampire life is changing so quickly that we need someone young like you to write it all down, to explain it, so future vampires will understand how and why we've adapted to living with humans.

"When I was first a vampire, we bit people and suffered horribly for that. We lived far from cities, in vast, dusty castles. Now we travel freely among humans and blend in so well, they don't know who we really are."

Gramps says I'm part of a new generation of vampires, one growing up with people, even going to school with them, seeing up close how humans work (and don't). But I'm not a historian. I'm a kid who's also a vampire. Or a vampire who's also a kid. He says that doesn't matter. If I write down my life and what I know about being a vampire today, I'll be doing an important job.

I don't know about that, but I promised him I'd try. So that's what I'm doing.

January 3

The problem is, my life is pretty boring. Since nobody at school can know I'm a vampire, it's hard to have regular, human friends. I certainly can never invite anybody over.

When I was younger, that didn't matter so

much, but now, in middle school, it does.

I suppose I should explain how vampires age. That's probably one of those things Gramps expects me to write about. But this is my diary and I'll get to that when I want to, which isn't right now.

Right now I want to write about the human world -- school, people, how to make friends. Because the thing is, I want to have friends. For me, that's the whole point of going to school. Well, that's not totally true. Sometimes I learn stuff. Right now we're studying ancient Egypt, and that's really interesting.

I bet there were vampires during the time of the pharaohs. I bet some pharaohs were vampires themselves They sure had vampire-like powers. They could turn themselves into animals, or part animals, like the Sphinx.

And they had this magical connection with cats, snakes, and crocodiles. Sounds vampire-ish to me. Plus everyone knows that the Egyptians invented the mummy and the mummy's curse. Which are vampire cousins for sure. So social studies is definitely interesting to me right now.

But my favorite part of school, the learning part, I mean, is science. I love it when we mix up concoctions, which we never do enough of. I love studying strange insects and the really bizarre things they do. Like spiders. They're like vampires, too, because they suck the blood out of their prey.

Last month we learned about a weird fungus that attacks ants in the rain forest and takes over control of their brains (okay, they're limited, tiny ant brains, but still!). They're actually called zombie ants, because that's what they are - ants controlled by a creepy fungus that hatches more funguses (or is it fungi?) from the body of the ant. Totally gross and totally cool!

Besides learning interesting stuff every now and then, the best part of school - and the worst - is the kids. Most of them totally ignore me. I don't know if it's because even without knowing I'm a vampire, they can tell I'm different, or if it's because I'm just bad at acting human. I used to be way worse at it. Once in kindergarten, I brought in a bunch of dead rats for show and tell. As you can guess, that didn't go over very well. But I'm much better about that kind of thing now. I don't blurt out weird stories about pet owls or great-Uncle Morris and his incredibly long eyebrows.

And when we learned about the zombie ants, I didn't say anything about meeting real zombies, even though I have and they're way more stupid than ants. I try to act as normal as I can, whatever that is. By now, in 6th grade, I think I'm finally convincing enough that I can try to make friends.

This year, for the first time, I've even found three boys I kind of like. We eat lunch together and hang out during class when we can. Which means they must like me, too, believe it or not.

Lucas -- smart, funny, has an amazing comic collection that he brings to school. He even let me borrow his Spiderman and Bone collection.

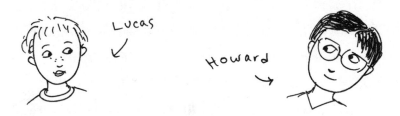

Howard -- super-good at video games, knows all the shortcuts and cheats. Ask him any question about the original Star Trek show and he knows the answer.

Joel -- smart in his own strange way, an expert on geography - if anyone knows where Kirghistan is (and how to spell it), he does. Great at sudoko and any other kind of number puzzle.

Joel →

I know what you're thinking - these guys are all nerds. But only in the best possible way. They brush their teeth and wash their hair, so they aren't total dweebs. Plus they're funny and smart and nice. They're fun to be with, human kind of fun.

I wouldn't call myself a nerd, though I suppose other kids might. Just because I don't fit into the usual social categories. I'm not a jock or artistic type or the kind to run for student council. I'm not a brainiac or jazz musician. I suppose that leaves nerd. Really I'm just "other." In every way possible.

COOL   DUNNO   NERD   OTHER   VAMPIRE

Mom says I'm going through my Ugly Duckling phase and soon I'll blossom into a handsome, dashing vampire.

Dad says I should learn judo or karate in case I don't.

Thanks, Dad.

You probably think because I'm a vampire, I have superpowers and that should make me supercool. The problem is, I can't show them off at school since nobody can find out I'm a vampire.

Plus my superpowers aren't the same ones that the vampires famous in history have. I'm not strong, but I can climb walls like Spiderman, and I'm great at jumping really high and really far. Too bad it's a family rule - No Sports Teams. It's part of the No Calling Attention to Yourself rule.

Problem is, if you're a boy and you don't play sports at my school, you're nobody. If only Dad would let me do track!

I can turn myself into a bat and fly, but you've probably already guessed doing that at school is a HUGE no-no. So I'm left with being as plain and ordinary and uncool as possible.

While I'm waiting to turn into the cool vampire that's hidden away inside of me, I have to survive 6th grade. Which is the first year of middle school. Which is the door to the Gates of Hades.

That means once you pass inside, you'll face all kinds of trials and tribulations. Middle School is tough on humans and non-humans alike!

January 4

It's hard to say what's the worst thing about middle school. Sometimes I think all the other boys are werewolves.

They growl and bark a lot - and that's when they're having fun, not even fighting. The only ones who really talk to me are Lucas, Howard, and Joel.

Oops, I shouldn't have said that! But really, compared to most vampires I know, I have a healthy tan because at least I'm outside a little every day. I had to think fast and say something that sounded normal and human-like, so they wouldn't think I was a total weirdo, but all I could think of was this:

"Gotta get home and feed my goldfish!" Which was totally lame. Who rushes home to feed fish?

Lucky for me, my nerd friends are almost as allergic to sunlight as I am. So when I don't play soccer or basketball, it's okay. They still eat lunch with me. You'd think that lunch would be the one place I would fit in. But you'd be wrong.

18

I'll tell you what's icky - cafeteria food. That's a whole higher level of absolute disgustingness. Nothing is actually food there. It's all over-cooked chemicals shaped to vaguely resemble something edible.

bumpy, crunchy chickenish bits

saucy, lumpy beefy bits

Raw liver is delish compared to that! Plus it's full of nice, tangy blood. I know some vampires only drink blood, but we're the kind that also eat, so long as what we're eating is plenty bloody.

Of course drinking is still the best. Mom always packs me a special juice box.

BLOOD
FRESH from
PLASMA
CONCENTRATE
TYPE A POS

Sometimes she gives me type O, sometimes AB negative or A positive. It's nice to have a variety.

Lucas saw me drinking some today and asked to taste it. Of course, he thought it was blood orange juice, the way he was supposed to, not plain blood.

I told him Mom gets mad if I share lunch stuff because she wants to know I'm getting all my vitamins. It sounded like something a human mom would say. Lucas bought it.

Problem was, I happened to say it right when Gertie was passing by with her vegan burger.

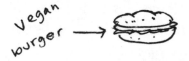

Vegan is like Vegetarian Plus. Those people eat nothing that has even gotten close to an animal. No butter, yogurt, cheese, milk, eggs, chicken, fish, pork, veal, goat, lamb, beef, hyena. Basically if it tastes good, they don't eat it. Know what they eat instead?

Vegetables! Talk about a weird kid! She's a girl who eats mostly green things, some brown (like wheat or rice), some grayish (like oatmeal), but nothing with any flavor or real color to it. Who chooses carrots over ice cream? Brussels sprouts over brownies?

You can guess that somebody like that doesn't look too kindly on liver sandwiches, raw or cooked. Gertie's been glaring at me for weeks now. Maybe because I make a tempting target since I'm not remotely popular. Maybe because of the way I dress or comb my hair or eat my lunch. Maybe it's the shoes I wear. But this was the first time she said something. Like she couldn't resist when she heard my lame-o excuse for not sharing my drink.

"Oooh, poor Edgar, little mommy's boy! Can't do anything to upset his mother, can he?"

"What did you say?" I wasn't sure how to respond. Can a human boy fight with a human girl? Can a vampire boy?

I need to stop here and explain something before I write down the rest of what happened or there's no way Gramps or anyone else will understand this. These are the facts about Gertie.

First, she's a girl, and girls travel in packs, worse than wolves even.

Second, she's a cool girl, the kind all the other girls want to be friends with, the kind all the boys have crushes on (even though she's a vegan which should make her totally repulsive). If she were a boy, not eating meat would automatically make her not cool. But as a girl, it somehow makes her even cooler, like she's a better person because she doesn't eat cows. Or their milk. Or things made from them, like chocolate, cake, pies, basically anything delicious.

To boys, eating meat is manly. To some girls, it's mean. To me, it's food, plain and simple.

Anyway, Gertie's had it in for me for a long time, though I don't know why she'd even notice me. We're so far apart on the school social scale, it's like we're breathing different air. But today, it was as if for her to feel like she was really on top, she needed someone to really be on the bottom.

23

Guess who that someone was?

I wasn't an Ugly Duckling waiting to transform into a swan, like Mom said. I was a scapegoat, a convenient target. Usually she was content with snotty comments. Today she was ready to attack. Maybe another girl had insulted her, maybe she'd fought with her mom that morning. Who can understand the motivations of humans? All I knew was that I was in the wrong place at the wrong time, about to be swept up in a furious Gertie storm.

"I said you're a big baby!" That wasn't so bad, but she followed that with throwing her garbage down on the table in front of me. Then another girl tossed her trash down, and another, and another. Until a big, stinking pile reached almost to my nose.

"Think you're so tough with all that horrible meat you eat? You're just a creepy animal bully. A total loser!"

I was wondering who was the real bully here, but nobody else was. Once she called me a loser, my fate was sealed. Everyone would be saying it. After all, they were thinking it before. Gertie was just encouraging them to take their disdain a notch higher. Or would that be a notch lower?

She flounced off, followed by her girl pack.

I sat there, like the social misfit I was, one rung further down in the pecking order, while she was one rung even further up.

Lucas, Howard, and Joel all stared at me, like I'd savagely bitten an innocent lunch lady.

"I didn't do anything!" I said. "I was just eating my sandwich, drinking my juice."

They still stared at me.

I rolled my eyes. Even my sort-of friends weren't backing me up. Where was all that human loyalty, those ties of friendship, I'd read so much about?

"I get it," I said. "You don't want to be seen with me anymore. Now that I've been cursed by Gertie, nobody will come near me."

"Hey," Lucas blurted out. "That's not true! We're not fans of Gertie, either. But vegetables ARE good for you."

"We're still your friends," Howard said.

"Don't worry about it," Joel added. "By tomorrow the whole thing will be forgotten."

"Really?" I asked.

"Well, maybe." Joel sounded hopeful but not at all sure.

26

I wanted to be so cool, no one like Gertie could ever insult me, so cool even she would have a big crush on me, so cool everyone would want to be my friend.

There was only one way I could think of to be that cool - if kids knew I was a vampire. It made me want to climb the walls right then and there - that would show them!

But I didn't. How could I? My parents would kill me. I don't mean really kill me. Obviously, I'm undead so I can't die, but you know what I mean. I'd be grounded for life and for a vampire, that's an eternity.

January 7

The rest of the week was as bad as I'd dreaded. Clive, the football jock, tripped me accidentally-on-purpose. A girl threw spitballs at me during science. And somebody shoved garbage in my backpack.

I was the school scapegoat now. The kid everyone hated. And Gertie was the school hero, the kid everyone loved.

First a Duckling, now a Goat. What next, a werewolf?

I have to give Lucas, Howard, and Joel credit. They stuck by me like they said they would. Joel even seemed embarrassed that the whole thing hadn't blown over.

That part was actually good. I felt like they were more than sort-of friends now. They were real friends, my first ever.

January 8

I was eager for the weekend, for all the hassles to finally stop. But I forgot that meant no more hassles AT SCHOOL. Saturday is something else entirely - it's the day I always get treated like freeze-dried sludge. Not by other kids. By other vampires.

Some families go to church or synagogue or the mosque on the weekend. Not us. We go to the Saturday Vampire Jamboree, also known as Pick-on-Edgar Picnic.

Because if the kids at school think I'm a loser, my vampire cousins have an even lower opinion of me. To them, I'm a nerdy, dorky vampire, an insult to the entire vampire race.

I told my parents I had a headache. I told them I had so much homework, I had to stay home and do it. I told them I had a sore throat and a toothache. Maybe I tried too many excuses, because they didn't believe any of them.

So Saturday as soon as the sun set, we drove to Grandfather and Grandmother Rakula's house. Lots of cars were driving up at the same time and some horse-drawn carriages for the more old-fashioned vampire relatives.

For some reason, there's always lightning flashing over their house

Mom's parents are classic, creepy vampires, the kind you see in old black-and-white movies.

Dad's are a strange mix of vampire and Midwestern comfortable.

always knitting bat booties →

Granny Stoker →

Pick a card!

Any card!

always practicing hokey card tricks ↙

← Gramps Stoker

My uncles, aunts, and cousins are a big blend of styles, but they all have one thing in common - they're cool vampires, the kind everyone admires, fears, and respects. Even regular people who don't know they're vampires can tell there's something special about them. In other words, they're the opposite of me.

You can see why I don't fit in.

As soon as we got to the Rakula house, Mom went to the kitchen to mix up the blood cocktails. Dad went to the library to help Grandfather with his collection of incunabula. I think that's an amazingly cool word - incunabula. Doesn't it sound like some kind of Creature of the Night? What it really means is a book, an early printed book, like from the 15th Century. Grandfather specializes in books about vampire folklore and the 15th century was big on the subject.

I keep promising myself I'll use that word in conversation one day, but I can never figure out quite how.

Then I could laugh and explain what incunabula really means. I wonder if I tried it on Gertie, would she'd think I was cool? Or even nerdier? Humans are so hard to figure out!

Normally at Jamborees I hang out with the little vampires because they look up to me. I'm great at organizing games of bat-tag and wall-climbing. But I'm in middle school now, I have a few human friends, and that gave me the courage to go up to a group of cool, older cousins.

Big mistake! Vampires don't say howdy. Nobody does. I don't know what possessed me to say such a dumb thing. A banshee or a ghoul probably. They made me say it.

banshee →

a female spirit, usually seen as an omen of death ←

ghoul →

an undead spirit known to haunt graveyards and eat human flesh ←

← Not my friends! →

The cousins ignored me, like they always do.

Elvira ↙

Elvira – She's a junior in high school, wears tons of make up, and her main expression is of total boredom. She's been everywhere, done everything, and says nothing new will ever happen to her again. The main reason for that is she's been the same age for three centuries now. She's one of those Peter Pan vampires, the kind that don't want to grow up. I tell her that she should try aging like I do. She'll have new experiences that way, but she says that the times (and fashions) changing is enough novelty for her. I can't imagine an eternity of high school! That takes a strong stomach, so Elvira must be tough, even if she moans about boredom. Eventually, when she's finally had enough, she'll age up a year, but for now she says the only thing she has to look forward to is the senior prom, so she's holding off as long as she possibly can.

Elvira through the ages
↓

Veronique - She's a senior in high school and is the artiste of the family. I say artiste and not artist, because she's got this attitude that goes beyond making art. She claims her whole life is a work of art. Her hair certainly is! I have to give her credit, though, she's willing to age and has only been in high school for a decade or so. She keeps changing schools so nobody notices that she hasn't graduated yet. She says she blew it by not aging into a twenty-year-old in 1930s Paris (before WWII, of course). That was the time to be an artist, and she missed it. Instead she was in elementary school in Milwaukee then - what a let-down! She swears she won't make that mistake again and is waiting for the next brilliant art capital to emerge. Istanbul? Tokyo? Budapest?

Lucinda - She's in 8th grade, but not at the same middle school as me. She's smart and funny and completely sure of herself. I've tried to make her like me so many times and in so many ways, it's become a family joke. For example, How many Edgars does it take to light up one Lucinda light bulb?

None! She lights up all by herself and he just makes her go dork. (Dork, dark, get it?)

I know, I know, it's a dumb joke, not funny at all.

Zoe - She's also in 6th grade, at Lucinda's school. Which is fine by me because I think she's a spoiled brat. All she cares about are the latest clothes and hot brand names. You would think after a century or two, that kind of thing would get old, but she boasts about the Dior purse she has from the 1920s. So she bought it new and not at a vintage clothes store - big whoop!

She's the one cousin I don't care about being friends with. She boasts that she's one of the few vampires to live through middle school (I mean not skip over it entirely), and except for Lucinda and me, so far she's right. Which makes me the only boy brave enough to do it. I hadn't thought about that before.

There are only two boy cousins, both older (high school seniors) and both super-cool. Which means they barely even look at me. Every Jamboree, I study them and try to figure out what makes them so amazing and how I can be like them.

Besides growing tall, handsome, and muscular, there have got to be things I can imitate. Only so far I haven't figured out what.

Barnaby with
his bat tattoo
→

Barnaby doesn't talk much, but he doesn't

need to. Mostly he makes quick, sharp comebacks. Sometimes I think his silence makes him seem smarter than he really is. If you want to seem profound, just nod your head and look like you have some deep understanding that's so mysterious you can't express it. Other times I think he's scarily clever because he'll mention some strange fact that only somebody who's read about a zillion books could possibly know, like how many feet above sea level Quito is or who first discovered that lemmings leap off cliffs into the ocean.

He's super-strong and fast, the way you'd expect a vampire to be. But like me, he's not allowed to show off at school, so no track team, no winning races. With him, that doesn't matter, because somehow just standing still, he seems powerful, like a coiled spring, tight with energy. How can I copy that? Maybe I should just try the strong, silent treatment. Or I suppose I could start reading more books.

Then there's Thadeus. He tells everyone he has the soul of a tortured poet. Meaning he sighs a lot. And sometimes he talks in rhyme, which sounds silly, if you ask me. Only he calls it Vampire Rap or Spoken V. Poetry. He has a lot of the same Boredom Pose that Elvira has and he's been a teenager even longer - 557 years, if you can believe that! But he talks much more.

His biggest skill is making lame poetry, if you consider that a talent. Sample rhyme:

It's tough to be a bat, a rat, a cat
 But more than that,
It's tough for me
To fit poetry
Into daily life
That's filled with strife
And a butter knife.

He's been writing poetry for so long, you'd think he'd be good at it by now. He says I don't understand Vampire Rap, and that if I did, I'd see what a genius he is. Since I don't, he thinks I'm a jerk.

Why can't he write like that poet who was a friend of his centuries ago, a weirdo human who was as close to a vampire as you can get? You know, the one who wrote about the raven and the creepy pit and the pendulum? Come to think of it, that guy was named Edgar, just like me, Edgar Allan Poe! Now he wrote great poetry!

With the cousins ignoring me, I ate with the little vampires. That meant wiping runny noses, telling silly knock-knock jokes, and playing with six- and seven-year-olds.

Which was fun for about three minutes.

At least at school, I have friends to sit with. I hate Saturday Vampire Jamborees!

I felt totally sorry for myself. Mom was wrong - I'd be an Ugly Duckling forever. And I mean forever because that's how long vampires live.

Of course, I could skip that phase and go right to Cool, Amazing Vampire Dude, so why don't I? Why do I choose to live as a 6th grader? I'd like to think I'm being courageous, that I'm willing to face the full adventure of middle school. That I'm braver than Thadeus and Barnaby since they went right from age ten to eighteen. Being a middle-school vampire is my one way to be unique in a good way, a vampire who counts for something.

Or maybe it's like Gramps says, we're so used to living among humans, we want to be like them, even if that means aging the same way they do.

Anyway, back at the Jamboree, Thadeus was spouting more poetry.

"Wait! I can feel it! Inspiration is here!"

The moon is low, the day is near.
It's time to go and swallow fear.

Fear tastes yummy!

    Doesn't that sound like "One fish, two fish, red fish, blue fish" to you?

    I asked Thadeus what he was afraid of, and he glared at me. So Veronique answered for him.

    "How can you understand?" she snapped. "Don't even try!"

    Zoe and Lucinda fluttered their eyelashes like sick cows.

    "What a genius!" they cooed.

I can't imagine girls ever going goo-goo eyed over me. Like I said, it's not fair.

It's one thing to be invisible at school, it's another to be scraping the floor of the Vampire cool scale. If I'm not careful, my cousins will start calling me a zombie. That's the worst of the worst. Maybe you think all the Undead play well together, but that's not true. If there's one thing vampires despise, it's zombies.

Here's why: zombies WERE dead - they're just brought back to life, usually with voodoo or some kind of nasty witchcraft. Vampires are immortal. That is unless someone stabs us with a wooden stake. Things like garlic, holy water, and crucifixes can weaken us, but not much can kill us. You can kill zombies a million different ways. There's really nothing special about them.

And everyone knows zombies are DUMB! That's why they're always trying to eat your brain - because they don't have one.

Don't confuse zombies with mummies, another creature that was human, died, and came back to life.

In their case, it's the mummy's curse that gives them power. But they can be killed in the same ways zombies can. Plus they're nowhere near as strong as us vampires. The only thing they have going for them is that they're way smarter than zombies. And they're known to be great dancers.

So I'd pick a mummy friend over a zombie any day.

Legend has it that 100 years or so ago, a vampire invited a zombie to the Saturday Jamboree. BIG MISTAKE!! The zombie couldn't play any games or dance or turn into a bat. It just sat there, like the blithering idiot it was.

Then it tried to eat a vampire. Not a real threat, of course, since vampires are so strong and a zombie's rotten teeth are nothing like a wooden stake. But still, it was a rude thing to do.

My great-grandfather whacked it with a shovel, and it's buried behind the house here. They even put a nice marker on the grave, which was more than the stupid zombie deserved.

So now it's a rule - No Zombies Allowed. Werewolves, witches, wizards, ghouls, mummies, and demons are okay in theory, but I haven't seen any of those at a Jamboree, either. It's just us vampires and has been for many years.

January 9

I was just waiting for it to be time to go when Grandfather struck the great gong twelve times. BONG BONG BONG BONG BONG BONG BONG BONG BONG BONG BONG BONG! (Count them if you don't believe me - they're all there, all 12 bongs.)

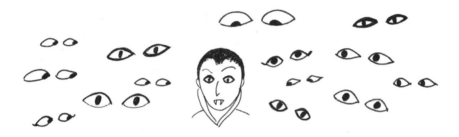

That meant all eyes on Grandfather. Every Jamboree ends the same way. Grandfather instructs us with Words of Immense and Ancient Wisdom (I told you vampires are smart), and then we all drink the Potion of Daylight.

Grandfather has a creaky voice, like the lid of a coffin squeaking open. His accent is thick and dark, kind of like snarling dogs. He's from the Old Country and his specialty is Stories from Days Long Ago and Far Away.

When I was little, I loved to listen to him. But today, at the end of a boring Jamboree after a horrible week, I couldn't.

Somehow tonight Grandfather sounded just like my math-science teacher, Mr. Kett. The same gravelly drone, like a motor putt-putting in the background, the kind of tuneless murmur that puts me to sleep.

Next thing I knew, someone had jabbed a sharp elbow right into my ribs. OUCH!

The elbow was connected to Zoe, the brat.

"Have some respect!" she hissed at me.

"Thanks," I snapped. "I'd love some."

"Idiot!" Zoe sneered and stomped off. Not very respectful, if you ask me.

"And that is why we must be ever alert to the enemy," Grandfather was saying. "Vampires must endure. The earth depends on us - we are her beating heart!" Grandfather shook his finger, his favorite gesture. "We can't allow these rumors to spread. Mortals can't know that we're more than nightmares that roil their sleep. So be aware and be more careful than ever that no one learns our true identities."

I had NO idea what he was talking about. What rumors? Did people suspect somebody was a vampire? Had a cousin bitten a dog in public again?

hot dogs — a favorite vampire snack →

I would have asked Zoe-of-the-sharp-elbow but I couldn't see where she'd gone. And I didn't want another jab anyway.

Instead I got in line for the Potion.

As vampires, we've learned to adapt to the human world. One of the most important skills we've developed is how to survive daylight.

One weekly dose of Sun-B-Gone, invented by my great-grandmother, Morticia LaBelle von Dead, and you can be out in the sun for seven full days with no ill effects. Before Sun-B-Gone, it was hard to have much to do with regular people unless you worked a night job, like at a 24-hour convenience store or in an emergency room.

And vampires are curious about mortals. We like them and not just because they're tasty. Humans are interesting. Maybe because they can die, they seem much kinder than vampires generally are, more sensitive. Which doesn't mean there aren't mortal brats and bullies. Sure there are. But there's a sweetness to people that's touching. It's hard to explain. But it's one reason I have three human friends -- they're nicer to me than most of the vampires I know so much better.

53

Back to the Potion. Before Morticia figured out the secret ingredients, the only way to mix with humans was at night. But going to bars, nightclubs, hospitals, and all-night stores only allows you to meet a certain kind of person. For one thing, hardly any kids (except sick, hurt ones at the hospital). For another, the grown-ups are often drunk, sleazy, or truckers driving all night. Not the best mix of types, though at least you could go to the movies. The midnight show is still my favorite.

So Sun-B-Gone has given us a lot of freedom, a whole new way of living with people. The only thing is - and this is important - you have to drink a full dose. Everyone knows the story of Cousin Boris.

It was the end of the Jamboree, and Boris was having a great time.

"Let's dance some more! It's not dawn yet!"

Except he had the hiccups. Even as he drank - hic - the Potion.

Boris was annoyed by the hiccups (they are pesky, aren't they?), but didn't think much about them until the next day.

He strode out into the morning sun to go to his job at the Blood Bank where he was a nurse. Nobody is better at drawing blood than vampires, believe me! We always know how to find a vein.

"What a beautiful day! After such a beautiful night!"

Then he hiccuped – hic! And fainted dead away.

He came to, but kept on hiccuping and with each hiccup, he got weaker and weaker. Until the last hiccup, when he fell down DEAD.

I know, I know, vampires are the Undead. How could Boris die? If you're up on your vampire lore, then you know that there are two things that can kill a vampire.

A wooden stake, right through the heart.

And sunlight.

Contrary to what you may have heard, garlic doesn't kill vampires, though it does gross us out. Can't stand it really, so it keeps us far away. That's why Italian food isn't popular with my family.

And it's also why Mr. Duncan, the P.E. teacher, is my sworn enemy. Besides being a typical bossy, out-of-shape-himself gym teacher.

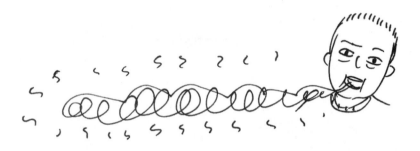

Coffee and garlic breath combined - what could be worse?!

Back to Boris. The Sun-B-Gone potion counteracts the deadly effects of sunlight, but with Boris, the hiccups kept him from getting the full dose. And each time he hiccuped in the bright light of day, he got weaker and weaker and weaker. Until the impossible happened.

So *believe* me, I was **WIDE** awake and totally careful the way I always am when it was my turn to drink.

I just wish it didn't taste so disgusting! Kind of like vampire mouthwash, the really nasty industrial-strength kind, used to remove all blood traces.

The only thing that gets rid of the Potion taste is a quick slug of blood, so there are always cups of it poured out for us to gulp down after the Potion.

Now my great-grandmother is working on some kind of anti-stake vaccine. She hasn't gotten it right yet, but I'm sure she will someday. That's one advantage of being immortal - there's plenty of time to learn from your mistakes and get things right.

Then she says she'll deal with crucifixes and garlic. I bet by the next century, we'll be totally invincible.

We're already better than the other super-naturals (zombies, werewolves, witches, all those guys), but with her help we'll be Rulers of the Living and the Undead forever!

That Jonas Salk had some interesting ideas. The Einstein fellow, too. There's something about gravity, wood density, applied force — I've just got to figure it all out...

I tell her that while she's at it, add some type A negative blood flavoring. Might as was well invent a delicious vaccine instead of a yucky one.

Here's another little known fact about vampires, at least those in my family. While we can't die (except for the two causes you've already heard about), we can get older. If we want to. It's entirely a choice thing.

We have a potion for that, too, also developed by -- who else? -- my great-grandmother. I told you, she's one smart cookie!

Most vampires decide to stay in their 30s, like my parents, my great-grandparents, my great-

great-grandparents, and my great-great-great-great-great grandparents (yep, they're all still around since they're immortal). But some choose to grow older, like Granny and Gramps. Granny says that after you've been 32 for three centuries, you're ready for a change.

The Aging Potion is the reason you rarely see baby vampires. Like Mom says, who wants an immortal, crying poop machine? Better to go right to an age you can reason with, say four or five, in one quick gulp. Plus that way you can skip diapers entirely!

So that's another thing that happens at the end of each Jamboree. If you want, it's your chance to drink some Aging Potion.

Tonight I'm actually tempted. Usually I take one teaspoon every June, so when school starts in the fall, I'm the same age as the rest of my class. But now I wonder, why not skip middle and high school altogether and go straight to being a grown-up? I could turn into that handsome, dashing vampire Mom's always talking about. No more Ugly Duckling! No more Scapegoat!

me as a cool guy, all in one sip!

63

But I don't. I can't. Not yet. How can I give up on middle school when I've only been going for a few months? I mean, if regular human kids can survive middle school, why can't I? I can! I will!

Because even if some people think I'm a doofus, I know I'm not. I just have to show them the real me. Without, of course, showing them the real me.

I'm walking a narrow line this way

It's tricky to show I'm strong, but not too strong. Fast, but not super-fast. Clever, but not brilliant. But I'm a vampire - if anyone can pull it off, I can! And if I can be popular among humans, I won't mind so much that my vampire cousins ignore me.

The horrible night was finally over, and we got in the car to drive home, but Dad wouldn't let me lay down in the coffin, like he usually does. That's always my favorite part of the whole Jamboree, and now I didn't even get that! This was the crummiest week ever.

And it got worse.

"Sit up front with your mother and me," Dad said. "We need to talk."

Uh oh. It's always bad news when a parent says something like that, and vampire parents are no exception. Wanting to talk is bad. Needing to talk is terrible!

For all the talk of talking, there was a long, awkward silence.

Mom was the one who finally broke it.

"Edgar, dear, your father thinks that you've reached the age. . ."

"It's time for you to know about the Bats and the Rats!" Dad blurted out.

No, not that, the Dreaded Bat-Rat talk! No kid wants to hear this, ever!

I kept my hands over my ears and sang "100 Bottles of Blood on the Wall" all the way home. When Dad turned off the engine in our garage, I finally dared to stop. Was it safe? Dad stared at me. His usually chalky white face was bright pink. Could he be as embarrassed as me?

When he saw I could hear him, he looked down and mumbled an apology.

"Don't worry, Edgar, I won't say another word. I'll spare both of us."

Phew! That was close!

This morning, when I went to bed, I found a book on my pillow.

I told myself I wasn't going to read it – NO WAY! But I couldn't help wondering if there were some vampire secrets I really should know, like if I turn myself into a bat too many times, will I not be able to switch back someday? And how close to garlic can I get without passing out? Considering Mr. Duncan's nasty garlic breath, that's essential information. What about crucifixes? If they're broken, are they still powerful, and how much damage can they do to a strong vampire anyway?

Those were things I should know, and a book isn't like a parental talk. You can shut it whenever you want, you can read certain parts and skip others, and, most of all, a book can't embarrass you!

I ended up reading most of it that morning. Here are some of the useful things I learned.

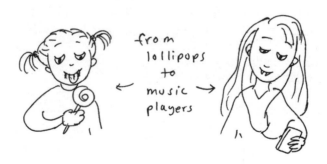

from lollipops to music players

1) Most vampires age from ten to sixteen, skipping the middle part. Only the bravest souls face those years. That way they go straight from pinatas and jump houses to driver's licenses and

the need to shave. For guys, we can skip the annoying voice cracking and go straight to deep, manly baritones in the blink of an eye.

You would think that would make me want to drink the Aging Potion at the next Saturday Vampire Jamboree, but it did just the opposite.

I want to be unique, a pioneer, one of the few vampires who faces the middle school and early high school years with grit and determination.

Maybe that's more important than being cool. Instead I can chart new territory - the Life of a Middle School Vampire.

One small step for me, one giant leap for vampires everywhere! Maybe that will make my cousins finally appreciate me and see how cool I really am. I bet Zoe is a coward and totally skips the next decade.

2) Another thing I learned is that there IS an antidote for garlic! This will be super-useful and make P.E. much more bearable. It's so simple -- ordinary, every-day parsley. You know, that green stuff that decorates plates in restaurants but no one actually eats. I just have to stuff my shorts, socks, and pockets with parsley, and I'll be fine.

If anybody asks, I'll say it's a natural deodorant— a green one! → Hah!

3) There's a reason vampires despise zombies, besides the obvious fact that they're blithering idiots.

Zombies exude a particular smell, part dried maggots, part foot fungus, part who-knows-what. To humans, it's disgusting, but to vampires it's absolutely nauseating. Evidently a vampire can't be near a zombie without getting the heaves.

That's why anti-zombie kits always include these.

Which makes me wonder why any vampire would invite a zombie to the Saturday Jamboree. Maybe the zombie crashed the party and wasn't invited at all. Makes more sense.

I didn't finish the whole book, but I read a lot of it. Not that I said a word to Dad about it. He didn't mention it, either. In fact, it was a perfectly ordinary Sunday.

Mom and Dad worked in the garden. There's a whole section of great herbs - henbane, hemlock, poison ivy, poison oak, and some oregano.

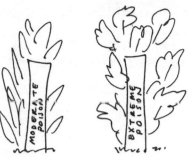

Me, I played Zombie Slaughter with my human school friends online. It's our favorite game and we're pretty good at it. So even though I can't have kids over to our house, I can still kind of be with them on the weekends and after school.

My screen name is *Proto Powerful Dude.*

Lucas is *Blaster Beast.*

Joel is Fearsome Force.

And Howard is Make-My-Day Harry.

Now that I know more about real zombies, the game is even more satisfying. I wish I could tell Lucas, Howard, and Joel about their nasty stink and raging stupidity, but I can't. They'd ask me how I know so much and that's a question I can't answer.

After hours of Zombie Slaughter, I almost forgot that tomorrow is Monday, which means school, which means more of Gertie's nasty insults. It'll be like the Saturday Vampire Jamboree all over again, only this time it will be mortals jabbing me with their elbows and telling me how dumb I am.

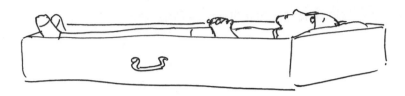

Maybe I should just stay home.

January 10

Lame excuses didn't work for not going to the Jamboree and they didn't work any *better* for not going to school. Mom practically pushed me out the door.

I dragged my feet, but somehow I still got to school on time. As soon as I walked through the front gate, it started. Someone threw a ball at me. Someone yelled out, "Hey, Dweeb, stop uglifying the school!" Someone else moaned, "The stink! The stink! The horror!"

Gertie stood right in front of me, blocking my way.

"Go home, Edgar. You're not welcome here until you stop your bloody meat-eating."

I clenched my fingers so hard, my nails gouged my palms. I wanted so much to bite her stupid neck and make her shut up! But I didn't. Biting humans is SO not allowed! If you really have to drink living blood, then find a dog or cat, a squirrel or chipmunk. Even a hamster is okay. NEVER touch a human if you don't want raging crowds going vampire crazy.

75

Joel crossed the hall in front of me, looking scared. He didn't say a word to help me. Howard came in behind me. He was too nervous to do anything, either. I knew Lucas would act the same way. And I couldn't blame them. I'd probably do the same thing if the situation were reversed. I couldn't count on anyone sticking up for me.

Except myself.

"You can't tell me what to do or what to eat! I don't make fun of your veganism, your eat-only-green-things extremism. What gives you the right to force your diet on everyone else? And is this really about food anyway?"

I wanted to say that being nasty to someone didn't make her more important or powerful or more popular - she was already all those things. Why did she have to be so snooty, so better-than-you-ever-could-imagine-yourself-to-be? But I knew if I mentioned popularity, I'd only enrage her more. Veganism was one thing, the P-word another.

   "Because I'm taking care of the planet and living creatures, and you're not!" Her voice was shrill and her face was red. She looked like a fire-cracker about to explode.
   "You're evil!" she shrieked. "A waste of space!"
That did it! I snapped.

I got mad, vampire mad, as in fangs and all. It's the way vampires look right before they sink their teeth into their prey and, believe me, it's terrifying. Even if the vampire is in 6th grade. Even if the vampire is me.

The bell rang and I realized what I was doing. Holy liverwurst, I was in trouble! Did Gertie think I was a vampire or just crazy? Either way, it wasn't good.

"Gertie, I'm sorry. Are you okay?" I said, back to my normal self. "You're right about vegetables - they're great for you. And I'm so glad you're taking care of the planet. I'm thinking about becoming a vegetarian myself." I was really babbling now, spouting all kinds of nonsense.

"Oh, Edgar, I've seen the real, true you! I promise I'll keep your supernatural secret. Only I can know that you're a. . ."

The late bell rang. Did Gertie really know I was a vampire? Could she really keep a secret? Was I in deep doo doo or what?

I rushed off to class. Maybe everything would be okay. Maybe Dad wouldn't lock me in my coffin for the next ten years. Maybe I could go back to being invisible, the kid nobody notices. I was so worried that my parents, my grandparents, the whole vampire clan would be furious with me, I couldn't pay attention to anything at school. Granny was yelling at me in my head.

"Edgar, how could you? You've broken the trust of every vampire! How can we have such a traitor in our family?"

Even worse was Grandfather's voice.

"I told you, the mortals must never know the truth of our existence! We must quash rumors, not start them. How could you have been so puny and weak as to lose your temper with a silly human girl? Where's your vampire dignity?"

I could feel him staring at me in vampire disapproval.

I couldn't blame them for being mad. I'd done the one thing a vampire should never do, reveal their true self to a mere mortal. And now only one thing could save me - if Gertie really could keep a secret.

What were the odds on that?

I studied everyone, trying to guess if they knew anything about me. It was weird. Everyone was looking at me, but no one would look me in the eye. I had a creepy feeling about this. By lunch, even the 8th graders were staring at me. That was a BIG sign that something was wrong. What 8th grader pays ANY attention to a 6th grader?

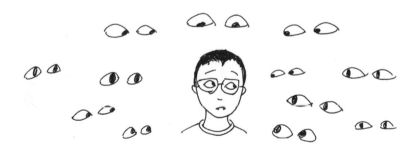

I sat down with Joel, Howard, and Lucas, like every other day. But it wasn't like every other day. I could practically feel the vibrations of their nervousness radiating through the lunch table.

For once, I felt self-conscious taking out my blood juice box. My bloody rib sandwich seemed to scream "Vampire!" I wrapped my lunch back up in its plain brown paper bag.

"I'm not hungry today." I shrugged.

Lucas stared at me, clutching his throat, his face paper white. "Are you thirsty?"

"Is it true?" Joel blurted out. "You're a vampire?"

"Who says so?" I demanded, though I knew exactly who.

"It's all over the school," Howard said.

Oh, Edgar, why are you eating with those losers? Come sit with me!

Please, pretty please!

Gertie looked exactly the same way Zoe and Lucinda did when they were around Barnaby and Thadeus.

Then it struck me.

I was cool!

Of course I was! Being a vampire is totally cool. I knew I wasn't supposed to spill the beans, that being a vampire was Top Secret Classified Information, but was it so terrible if some kids thought I was a vampire, so long as I didn't admit to being one?

It turned out I didn't have to say anything anyway. Gertie did all the talking. Thanks to her, even my teachers looked at me differently.

In social studies, Ms. Jewel was talking about immigration, how most Americans came here from somewhere else. She called on me, something she's never done *before*.

"Ahem. . . Edgar, why don't you tell us where your family came from?"

She sounded really nervous. I didn't want to disappoint her, so I smiled a big toothy grin.

"From Transylvania. Home of Dracula!"

I tried to imitate Grandfather's accent as best I could. I think I did pretty good. I must have, because when I said "Dracula," three girls in the back row screamed. The girls who didn't shriek, gaped at me like I was a rock star or something. Was it really such a bad thing if people found out we were vampires? Nobody was grabbing torches or pitchforks. Nobody was scrambling for wooden stakes. Nobody was even brandishing garlic or crucifixes.

Maybe it was time for vampires to safely be vampires.

The rest of the day was like some kind of dream. Girls following me, teachers passing me in the hall with looks of interest, jock boys smiling at me and saying, "Hey, Dude!" As if they were curious about me. Me!!

When I thought it couldn't get any better, something truly amazing happened.

Hey, Edgar, wanna come over after school?

No one has ever invited me to their house. Not to birthday parties, not for a little kid play date. Not ever for anything.

I was so stunned, I didn't know what to say.

If you're busy, that's okay. Another time, maybe.

"No!" I yelped. "I'm not busy. I'd love to come!" I realized as soon as I said it, it wasn't a cool thing to say. I should have seemed bored, not excited. That's a nerd-dweeb-dork way to behave. Everyone may think I'm cool, but I still have to learn how to act cool.

Not that it seemed to matter. Lucas grinned and said, "Great!"

Except what would Mom say when I didn't come home from school like usual? What would she say about me going to a mortal's house? There are rules about these things, but to be honest, I hadn't paid attention to them since I was sure nobody would ever invite me over.

Something about jumping over welcome mats? Or eating them? Or setting them on fire? If only I could remember.

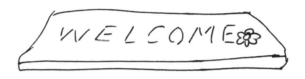

Even if I knew the rules, what would Mom say about kids knowing I'm a vampire?

I didn't want to think about that. It was so great being cool, even better than I imagined. Thinking about my family only soured a really good thing. So I didn't. Think about them, that is.

The rest of the day, I floated through school. It was the best day of my life!

I was at the very top of the social pyramid! Everyone wanted to be my friend, Gertie most of all.

"Ooh, Edgar! You have to eat lunch with me from now on, not those loser friends! Promise me, tomorrow for sure!"

It was a tempting offer, but the thing is, I really don't like Gertie, even if she is the coolest girl in 6th grade. Cool doesn't mean nice, or interesting, or a good friend, it's a whole other category. And I do like Joel, Howard, and Lucas. I figured I was so cool, I could eat lunch with any kid I wanted, and that meant NOT Gertie.

But all I said was, "Maybe" in my new, cool way.

After school, Lucas and I walked to his house. When we came to the front door, I racked my brain for what I was supposed to do about the stupid welcome mat.

"Are you coming in?" Lucas asked. "Come on,

let's get a snack."

I stared at the mat.

A minute passed. Then another.

"Edgar?" Lucas asked. He sounded worried, like I might change my mind and leave.

I had to do something. I couldn't burn or eat the stupid mat without looking like a crazy person, so I jumped over it.

I felt a huge wind at my back and then a stillness. I'd done it right! And I walked into my first mortal home ever.

Lucas gaped at me, but he didn't say anything. He just told me to leave my backpack by the front door, and we headed for the kitchen.

It was an ordinary human house, no skull lamps, no coffin beds, no huge black cauldrons brewing blood puddings in big stone fireplaces. And not a spider web or cobweb in sight! No dust even, the house was sickeningly clean!

Lucas poured himself a tall glass of milk and asked if I wanted some. It smelled so nasty, I had to cover my nose! School lunches were fine with their little individual milk cartons pierced by a straw, sealed up to keep in the curdling milk smell. In an open glass, the stench was overwhelming.

I had no idea what I'd been spared all this time! How can humans drink the stuff?

"Um, no thanks," I said to Lucas, trying to be polite.
"Oh, right, you only drink blood," he said.
"Blood orange juice," I corrected automatically.
"Yeah, right." He winked.
I didn't argue with him. After all, I wanted to be polite.

I waited until Lucas went to the bathroom to call Mom to tell her where I was. Good thing, too, because it wasn't a quiet conversation.

In fact, she went ballistic.

"You're where? At a human child's house? You know we can **NEVER** trust mortals. They can't be your friends. You're supposed to be part of the human world **WITHOUT** being part of it! If they knew the truth about you, they'd kill you, burn our home to ashes. And there you are, playing nice?!"

"Mom, you always say we have to fit in. That's what I'm doing, acting like a normal kid." I didn't add that she was wrong. Everyone at school thought I was a vampire now, and not only were they **NOT** mean to me, they were suddenly super-nice.

I told her I'd only stay an hour and she finally calmed down. That gave us enough time to go on the trampoline in the back yard and to play one game of Zombie Slaughter.

It was a perfect hour.

And then I had to go. "Sorry, but my mom will be mad if I don't get home soon," I explained.

"Is she a vampire, too?" Lucas asked.

This was getting tricky. I couldn't say yes because that would be breaking the Vampire Code of Honor. But if I said no, would he think I wasn't a vampire, either, and then I wouldn't be cool anymore?

The best thing was to say nothing. I grabbed my backpack and jumped back over the welcome mat.

"Thanks!" I yelled over my shoulder. "See you tomorrow!"

Once I was in the clear, I flew home as quickly as possible. But that didn't matter, Mom was still plenty steamed when I got there. So was Dad.

"Edgar, we need to talk!" he said.

Again with the needing thing about talking thing. A bad, bad sign.

"Listen to your father!" Mom said.

Another bad sign is when Mom says "your father" instead of "Dad." I could tell this would be a terrible talk.

Dad led me into his study, yet another bad sign.

I stared at the floor and nodded while Dad lectured me about the long history of humans hating and fearing vampires, how prejudiced they are against us, how we can only survive by pretending to fit in,

93

but we could never actually fit in.

Then he talked about how inferior mortals are anyway, so why be friends with them when I know so many wonderful vampires.

That's when I finally said something.

"That's great, Dad, but none of the cousins want to be my friend. They all despise me. For once, a kid liked me enough to ask me over. Is that so terrible?"

"That's not true!" Dad objected. "The cousins are very fond of you. If you'd give them half a chance, you'd see that."

There was no point in arguing with him over this. To him, my cousins were perfect. If we weren't friends, it had to be my fault.

I sighed. "Okay, Dad, you're right." I didn't believe it, but I said it so the lecture would be over. At least it satisfied Dad.

January 13

I didn't go over to Lucas' house for the rest of the week. And when Howard and Joel both asked me over, I said I couldn't. I figured I could do that much for my parents because the rest of the day, I loved being the cool vampire at school.

In the old days, before the vampire rumor started, if I did something Gertie didn't like, I'd find mud in my locker, have balls thrown at my back, end up with spitballs in my hair. Now not eating lunch with her, ignoring her even, just made her nicer to me.

It was weird. Are girls just opposite creatures, doing the opposite of what makes sense?

We talked about Gertie and her clique of friends, but Howard, Joel, and Lucas didn't understand them any better than I did. Being human boys didn't make them smarter about human girls.

So they couldn't tell me why every day there was a bigger group of girls surrounding us at lunch. By Thursday there was practically a mob.

Even weirder, some of my coolness was rubbing off on Howard, Lucas, and Joel. Some girls would call out their names. Others just smiled at them. I suspected that was one reason they all wanted me to come over. Not so much to be with me as to have everyone else see that I was with them, that I'd chosen them as friends.

I began to wonder if they liked me because of me or because everyone thought I was a vampire. Then I wondered if it mattered, so long as they liked me. The whole thing was getting very confusing.

But I'm not complaining -- it was still great.

January 14

By Friday, the girls did more than hover around me at school. They followed me home.

"He's so mysterious!"

"He's the most magnetic boy in school!"

"Think he'll notice me?"

"How can I make him like me?"

"Why are all those girls following you?" Mom asked. She sniffed like something smelled bad. "What's going on? First you go over to a human's house. Now humans come to yours. Something's fishy here!"

"Nothing's fishy!" I snapped. "Maybe I'm not an Ugly Duckling anymore. Maybe I've turned into a cool kid."

Moms are supposed to think you're special, wonderful, brilliant, even when you're not. Not my mom. She looked at me suspiciously.

"Edgar, there's something you're not telling me." She drilled me with her eyes. "I'm not just a vampire, I'm your mother. You can't lie to me."

After a week of keeping it all secret, I spilled the beans. All of them. I told Mom how mean Gertie was, how she pushed me until I couldn't help myself, I got mad, vampire mad. How she figured out I'm a vampire and told everyone in school. How great everyone's been since then, no angry mobs, just kids finally treating me with some respect!

"I never said I was a vampire. Never!" I insisted.

That part was totally true.

"But you never denied it," Mom pressed.

I shrugged. "If they wanted to think that, why stop them?"

"Because," Mom hissed, "there's a Vampire Code of Honor! You know that we have to keep our true identities secret. Every vampire in the whole international vampire clan has agreed to that."

She was right, and I was wrong, except things have changed. Maybe humans are ready to accept vampires now.

Mom sighed. "I know you didn't mean to cause trouble like this, Edgar. And maybe you're right about humans. But you can't decide on your own to change the rules."

"Then how do rules ever get changed?" I asked. "We've changed as vampires, deciding not to prey on people, things like that. Who decides? How?"

"Do you really want to do this? Is this so important to you?"

I nodded. I do. It is.

"There is a way," Mom admitted. "If you want to be known as a vampire, then present your request at the Jamboree tomorrow night. Maybe the others will agree with you."

"Do I have a chance?" I asked.

Mom shrugged. "You won't know until you try." She looked like she was trying to smile, but just couldn't manage it, so all she ended up with was a lip quiver. "And I'm proud of you for trying, even if I don't agree with you. Even if you're totally wrong."

Really? I took that as encouragement. And when Dad came home, he was actually calm about it.

I don't have the same faith in humans that you do, but, like your mother, I'm impressed you have the guts to suggest this. And people are definitely more tolerant than they were just twenty years ago. The question is, are they tolerant enough?

"Do you think the time is right, Dad? Are we ready for this? Are humans?" It sounded like neither of my parents agreed with me, but they were relieved I was willing to try. Did even my parents think I was a boring nerd? Did anyone believe in me?

"I don't know, it's been this way for so long, it's hard to imagine things changing. Besides, people are afraid of change, and so are vampires. I wouldn't get your hopes too high."

That answered my question - Dad didn't think I could make a difference. Mom didn't want me to.

How much chance did I have that the Saturday Vampire Jamboree would go my way?

I tried to give myself a pep talk, looking in the mirror, but of course that didn't work. I mean, I'm a vampire, so I can't cast a reflection. I can only listen to myself, which I did.

January 15

This time when we got to Grandmother and Grandfather's house, there was already a crowd standing in the front yard. I looked at Dad.

"Are they waiting for us? Did you tell them what I was going to propose?"

"I had to ask for you to be put on the agenda.

I tried to warn you this wouldn't be easy."

The crowd didn't look at all happy or welcoming. Why even bother to suggest being vampires in public? It looked like nobody would agree with me.

One thing you should know about me. I may not be popular. I may even be a nerd. But I'm stubborn, VERY stubborn.

I got out of the coffin in the back of the car, strode through that crowd, and went right up to Grandfather.

"May I speak first?" I asked.

Grandfather narrowed his eyes into slits. "I can tell you right now that you won't convince anybody."

"May I speak first?" I repeated.

Grandfather's eyes squeezed into lines of disgust, disdain, dis-you-name-it.

"So be it!" he snapped.

The crowd outside had followed us all into the house. There was a loud buzzing of voices, clinking of glasses, flapping of bat wings. And then silence as Grandfather struck the gong twelve times.

"Usually we end our Jamborees with Discussions and Instructions, Words of Wisdom to all. Tonight we begin the Jamboree with an Issue that one of us brings to the group for a decision. Here to present his position, I give you my grandson, Edgar Stoker."

There was no applause, but then no boos or jeers, either, just a thick, cobwebby silence.

I walked up to Grandfather, standing next to the great gong.

I need to pause here to note that people's number one fear, before disease, divorce, death, accidental dismemberment (Is there any other kind? Purposeful dismemberment?) is public speaking. That's right, talking to a crowd of people is more terrifying than a car accident, erupting volcano, or shark attack.

So if you can give a class presentation without shaking, you're an exceptional person. Vampires aren't human, but we have some of the same fears. We don't worry about being buried alive or bitten by a snake or struck by lightning. But public speaking is just as scary to us as it is to mortals.

Like I said, though, I'm stubborn. I cleared my throat and tried to speak as loudly and clearly as I could. This was no time to mumble or mutter. I had to be convincing or my life as a cool kid at school was over.

I told the story the way I'd explained it to Mom. I drew a picture of myself as a sad, lonely misfit, someone with a few friends but not much status at school. Then I described Gertie and her bullying behavior. When I said she was a vegan, the crowd booed. They booed!

The more detail I gave of all the juicy, bloody things Gertie wouldn't eat and all the drab green things she would, the more agitated they all become. Some shook their fists, others yelled out insults (to Gertie, not to me). I could feel they were all on my side now. Even Grandfather looked horrified as I talked about the Brussels sprout salad Gertie brought for lunch. And when she sneered at me for my raw liver sandwich, there was a loud chorus of "Down with Veggies! Down with Vegans!"

When I told how I couldn't take it anymore and got mad, vampire mad, there was an even louder cheer.

And then silence.

"I never said I was a vampire. Never!" I explained. "But when that girl saw my vampire fury, she recognized that I was one. And she told everybody in school."

Now the crowd was buzzing with questions, worries, fears, as though they expected a horde of humans to break down the front door with pitchforks. As if anybody even owned a pitchfork!

"It's okay!" I hurried to reassure everyone. I told them how it turned out that being a vampire was cool, not evil or scary. How nobody was mean to me and even the teachers treated me with respect. I ended by saying that the times had changed, and now we could be vampires openly without anyone wanting to shove a stake in our hearts.

"So let's vote on whether we can go public!

There's no reason to hide anymore, no more fear or prejudice against us. The Day of the Vampire is this day, right now!"

    Sploosh! Someone threw a glob of blood pudding right in my face. Splat! Someone else pelted me with blood sausages.

AAAAGGGHHH!!

"Get him!"
"He's a traitor to his race!"
"Make him shut up!"

Grandfather banged the gong until the ruckus quieted down.

"I take that to be your vote. No to being vampires in public. Our secret stays our secret. For eternity!"

Someone started up the music, and the party part of the Jamboree started. Nobody was looking at me anymore. I was back to being a nobody.

When Zoe came up to me, I thought she'd slug me. She looked like she wanted to.

"I can't believe you told the kids at school that you're a vampire!"

"I didn't! I just didn't tell them I wasn't one."

"Same difference!"

I shrugged. "It's different to me."

"You can't let them go on thinking you're a vampire. You're ruining it for the rest of us."

The vote had been against my idea that all of us could admit to being vampires. No one had said anything about denying being a vampire. Could I still be cool at school and not betray my family? Was it worth having humans like me if vampires hated me?

I didn't know what to do, but the rest of the Jamboree was bound to be horrible, even worse than usual.

Thadeus glared at me. Barnaby snorted his disgust. And the girl cousins all turned their backs as soon as they saw me near them. I was totally shut out.

I couldn't even play with the little kid vampires. They all seemed scared of me now. Their parents stared at me as if I were a horrible influence, threatening to bring evil human traditions, like Christmas, into their lives.

Stay away from Edgar — and don't listen to a word he says about humans!

The only vampire that came near me was Granny. "Now dear, don't take it so hard. It was a difficult thing you did, fighting against a tradition that's thousands of years old. It took a lot of courage."

Or a lot of stupidity.
"I'm proud of you, Edgar, always have been,"

III

Granny said. "And you should know you're not the first vampire to suggest we shed our secrecy and come out into the daylight. There have been others over the centuries, and there will be more in the future. The time simply isn't right yet. But one day maybe it will be."

"Who?" I asked. I'd never heard that part of vampire history. Maybe I should read more of Grandfather's books.

"The first was Cyrus the Bald, a Persian vampire who thought that the ruling class should be restricted to vampires. Makes sense really since we're stronger and much, much wiser than humans, given our personal knowledge of history. Cyrus wanted to divided Persia into Vampire Rulers, the Human Elite - that is the wealthier, educated humans - and the Slave class, the poor, stupid humans who would work for the rich ones and be livestock for us vampires. As you can imagine, that idea wasn't too popular. There was a huge vampire massacre, with Cyrus killed first. The humans no longer trusted supernatural creatures at all and slaughtered the Bull people next."

"But I'm not suggesting we go back to draining humans of their blood! Because we rely on blood banks and animal blood, we aren't a threat anymore. That's why people should accept us now!"

Granny shook her head. "The most recent attempt happened in early 20th century Paris. It seemed like the perfect age for vampires, with lots of night life. An exciting mix of all kinds of people, especially artists, came to experience the cultural richness of Paris. There was a tolerance for different tastes and experiences. Or so Gigi

LeNoir thought. She danced the can-can for artists like Picasso and Matisse.

"But when she whispered her secret to them, they called in the gendarmes and that was the end of Gigi. At least no other vampires were destroyed that time. You see, you can never trust humans. Never."

I knew she meant to make me feel better, but it wasn't working. I felt more alone than ever.

All around me vampires were dancing, drinking, laughing, and playing games. Bats flitted through the tree branches, vampire kids played zombie tag, old vampires sat together sharing stories and card games.

Why didn't I fit in? Here or anywhere?

I was staring at the dirt by my shoes when Zoe came up to me again. For more insults, I guessed. She wasn't finished yelling at me.

"Look, Edgar, I'm sorry," she said.

"What?" I couldn't believe I'd heard right.

"I'm sorry," she repeated. "Hey, I'm in 6th grade, too. I know what it means to be popular. And unpopular."

"You do?"

"Why do you think it's any different for me?" she asked.

"Because," I sputtered, "you're cool, not a loser like me."

"Maybe I'm cool here, with other vampires, but it's NOT like that at school, I guarantee you."

I stared at her. No way she was a total loser like me.

"I'm not at the bottom of the heap, but I'm nowhere near the top either. Kind of bottom of the middle. And that's okay. I don't want kids to notice me. It's safer to be invisible."

"But if the other kids knew you were a vampire, you'd be at the top of the pile!"

Zoe shrugged. "So what? It's not like I care what humans think of me."

Well, I do. I care a lot. Not that I would admit that to her.

Instead I said, "Okay, but who wants to be

bullied? Not me!"

"That's why I'm apologizing. I can see why you vampirishly blew up at that bratty girl. But you know what you have to do now."

I sighed. She was right. I did know. Somehow I would have to convince everyone the rumors weren't true, I wasn't a vampire. Starting with Gertie. But how?

"You know what would be great?" Zoe asked.

"What?"

"If you could get back at that mean girl and stop the vampire rumors at the same time."

"If I could get back at Gertie, it'd be worth stopping the vampire rumors," I said.

Gertie with juicy meat sandwich.

How do you make the most popular girl in the 6th grade suddenly unpopular? Is it possible?

It was an interesting challenge. Would it be

enough to prove that she was wrong when she told everyone I was a vampire? Would that make her look stupid or untrustworthy or simply ordinary? After all, humans make mistakes. There's even a saying, "to err is human." Nobody says, "to err is vampire." Which goes to show how superior we are, if you needed proof.

"If I think of anything, I'll let you know," Zoe said.

She was offering to help me? Was she trying to be nice? I was too stunned to say anything, but that was a definite first for a Saturday Vampire Jamboree - someone coming up to talk to me who wasn't Granny. And being nice about it.

January 16

By dawn, back home, I still hadn't thought of how to handle Gertie and the vampire rumor. I had one more day to figure things out. Tuesday was VRO Day - Vampire Rumor Over Day.

You know how you can try and try to think of something, like writing a story, but the paper stays blank, and you can't think of anything to say? The more you turn possibilities over in your head, the more stupid they all seem. Then right when you least expect it, when you aren't thinking of anything at all, you'll get an absolutely brilliant idea. That's how it was for me.

It helped that the timing worked out. It was mid-January, so not too far-fetched if I wanted to send a valentine to somebody. And I did, very much. The stores start stocking that stuff right after Christmas, so it was easy to find a big, red, lace-edged valentine, all gooey and lovey-dovey.

On the outside of the envelope I wrote "To Gertie" and inside the card, I slipped my school photo from the beginning of the year.

January 18

Now that I had the card, I was so eager to get to school on Tuesday, I practically flew there, even without using bat wings. I didn't have to wait long. As soon as I walked down the hall, Gertie came up to me, all fluttery eyelashes and simpering smiles. I smiled back and handed her the big pink envelope.

"Oooooh, Edgar! For me! How sweeeeeeeet of you!" she purred. She couldn't wait to tear it open. Before she could read the sentimental tripe of a verse, the photo fluttered out, drifting slowly to the floor.

"A picture? Your picture?" she asked, picking it up.

Please be smart enough to figure it out, I prayed. Don't be a total dodo head.

The pack of girls who follow Gertie everywhere clustered around.

"A photo?" shrilled one.

"A photo!" echoed another.

"A photo!" Gertie bellowed. So she wasn't an idiot. Phew!

"Edgar, what does this mean?" she yelled in my face.

"Can we talk about this in private?" I asked. I didn't want to completely embarrass her. Otherwise my plan wouldn't work.

Gertie glared at her entourage and they

scurried away.

"How can you be a vampire if there's a photo of you?" she demanded. "Everyone knows vampires can't cast reflections or be photographed!"

I wondered when she'd become such an expert on us. I bet she didn't know how we dealt with the sun or garlic. She certainly didn't know how we handled photos.

I'll let you in on a secret - here's how we do it. Once vampires started sending their kids to school, the dreaded school photo became a BIG problem. At first, the vampire kids stayed home on those days, but year after year after year, that began to look suspicious.

That's when Uncle Martin had a genius idea.
If every school photographer all over the country
were themselves vampires, the problem vanished.
Because whenever the photographers were supposed to take a vampire student's picture, they
marked the blank negative with the name and de-
scription. Then, back at the photo lab, a call was
put out to all the other vampire school photographers until a match was found. School photos never
look like the person anyway, so if the nose or chin
was a bit off, nobody noticed. A close enough like-
ness could always be found.

My school photograph obviously wasn't really
me, since as even Gertie knew, vampires can't be

photographed. It was Melvin P. Johnson of Sioux City, Iowa.

Melvin
P. Johnson

What Gertie didn't know, what no mortals know, is that thanks to vampire school photographers all over the continent (yes, in Canada, too), no vampire child ever has to miss school on *Photo Day*.

If you don't believe me, look closely at the photographers on your School Picture Days. Can you tell they're vampires?

Say "Cheeese!"

Back to Gertie, who was shoving the photo under my nose.

"You tricked me!"

"I never said I was a vampire. You did." I felt strangely calm in front of her boiling fury.

"Edgar, you're an even bigger loser than I thought you were!"

"You didn't think I was such a loser all last week," I reminded her. "Everyone saw you follow me around, all sugary and sweet."

"Not true! I'm never sugary and sweet!"

Actually, I agreed with her on that one, but she was definitely acting all goo-goo eyed, and she knew it.

"Listen," I said. "It's fine with me if you tell everyone I'm not a vampire. Your friends who saw the photo will, if you don't. But if you spread nasty rumors about me being a total loser creep, what does that make the girl who had a crush on me?"

Gertie gulped. She turned paler than my great-aunt Lucretia and that's saying something.

"I get it," she said, crumpling up the photo. "I won't say bad stuff about you any more. But I won't say good stuff, either. I'll ignore you, got that? Totally ignore you!"

"Fine with me." I held out my hand. "Shake on it."

January 24

I guess things are back to normal now. I'm not cool, but I'm not dog doo doo, either. Maybe I'm like Zoe, at the bottom of the middle level of the social pyramid. Like she said, not a horrible place to be.

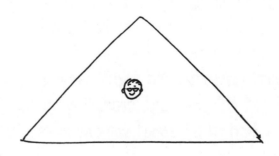

Howard, Joel, and Lucas are still my friends. And guess what? They still invite me over to their houses. Now that I'm not a known vampire, Mom lets me go, so long as I agree to NEVER invite them home. Besides, mortal feet can never touch our welcome bat.

They don't ask why I don't invite them over, and I don't offer any excuses or explanations. It's just the way it is. Nobody seems to mind. I know everyone says you can't trust a human, but in my experience, some of them make pretty good friends.

As for Gertie, she's as obnoxious as ever. But not to me. She's kept her promise, she totally ignores me. I can eat my juicy, bloody sandwiches in peace. No one puts trash in my locker. The jocks don't notice when I pass by. Sometimes it's good to be invisible, like Zoe said. The people who matter can always see you and who cares about the rest?

Sadly for Gertie, she's slipped a notch or two in the social hierarchy. She's not called a complete fool who had a crush on a loser, thinking he was a vampire. She's called an untrustworthy liar who spreads stories that aren't true.

"You can't believe a word she says!"
"I heard she called some kid a leprechaun."
"No, it was a werewolf."
"Uh uh, a zombie."
"Whatever! You can't believe her, that's all there is to it!"

Now I just have to see what happens at the next Saturday Vampire Jamboree when I announce that the vampire rumor is officially over. I wonder if I'll be a hero, the vampire who saved his clan? Maybe Barnaby and Thadeus will be impressed. Maybe Zoe will start liking me.

More likely, it'll be a Jamboree like any other and the only one to talk to me will be Granny. She's already told me that I did the right thing.

"Edgar, I'm so proud of you! Such a clever solution to a difficult problem! I knew you could do it."

I wish I had as much faith in me as Granny does. But I have all of middle school to figure out how to fit in - or not - in both worlds. All of middle school to figure out what really matters to me. And in the meantime, I'll make vampire history by writing it all down, so maybe one day, more of us vampires will stick out the middle-school years, just like humans. After all, if I can handle Gertie, I can deal with 6th grade.

I'll worry about 7th grade next year.

Edgar's Favorite
Chocolate Blood Pudding Recipe

Ingredients:
3 cups heavy cream
1 cup sugar
1 cup pig's blood
3 tbsp cocoa powder
1 tbsp pepper
3 sheets gelatin

Mix 2 cups cream, sugar, pig's blood, cocoa, and pepper in a sauce pan, and bring to a boil. Remove from heat and let sit for a while. Soften the gelatin in the last cup of cream for a few minutes, then strain the mixture from the saucepan and add the gelatin and cream. Strain the final mixture into ramekins or a muffin pan. Let them set in the refrigerator for 4 hours. serves 6. For a more tart flavor, substitute goat's blood. For added richness, try ram's blood and a pinch of nutmeg.